BEGGAR
BOY

BEGGAR BOY

Edgar J. Hyde

CCP

© 1998 Children's Choice Publications

Text supplied by Alan J. Henderson

ISBN 1-90201-208-9

Printed and bound in the UK

Contents

Chapter 1

I rolled the dice out of my hand onto the board. Oh no, a four and a six! I counted ten spaces around the board. I had landed on Regent Street, and it had a hotel on it! I counted the spaces out again but I still had landed there.

"You can count it as many times as you like, Tommy, but you are on my property," said Mum. "Let's see now. Regent Street with one hotel – that's a fortune!" she squealed with delight.

A quick glance around the Monopoly

board and at my Mum's pile of cash confirmed what I thought. I had lost to her again.

I looked at my meagre pile of cash and said, "That's me, I'm cleaned out."

"I win, I'm the champ!" cried Mum, as she shook her hands above her head in a victory salute. I may have been a bad loser, but she was an even worse winner!

"What are you going to do now Tommy?" she inquired. "It's a lovely day out there. Why not go out to play?" she added.

"Oh, I'm happy enough here," I explained with a faint smile.

Mum frowned and said, "Look Tommy, thirteen-year-old boys shouldn't be indoors keeping their Mum company on beautiful days like today."

"I know," I replied. "It's just . . ." I couldn't find the words to finish the answer.

Chapter 1

Mum put her arm around my shoulders and quietly said, "Are you still finding it difficult to make friends around here?"

I nodded my head with a feeling of embarrassment at my failure to make new friends. I had tried but around here it wasn't easy. The kids and even the parents called me "beggar boy".

We moved to this rich neighbourhood a few months ago. This was just after my sister, Emma, was born. Dad left us before the birth and has not been in contact since. I often wonder how he could be so cruel to treat us this way. Mum explains that we're, "Better off without him."

Dad left Mum with a lot of money problems. She couldn't keep up the rent in the flat because she couldn't go out to work because she had to look after Emma. In the end we had to move out and ended up in a local authority hostel, which was horrible. The bedsit in the hostel was cramped and smelly. Mum couldn't sleep at night for fear of us getting burgled, and the other occupants of the hostel frightened us.

Then our luck changed and we ended up here in the prosperous part of town. We occupy the garden flat of Mrs Benson's huge house in Montague Street. My granny used to be Mrs Benson's house-keeper, and they got along very well. My granny passed away a few years ago and, by chance, Mrs Benson found out about our circumstances, and offered us the garden flat. Mum couldn't say no to a chance like that.

In return for staying in the flat, Mum cleans the house for Mrs Benson. The house has three levels, plus the garden flat. This means there is a lot to clean, but this suits Mum as she can carry Emma along with her as she goes about her duties. So although we have a place to stay, we still have very little money. Mrs Benson pays very little after the rent is taken off Mum's wages. This is where my problems begin.

The area we now stay in is very wealthy. Everyone has a huge house and fancy cars. The kids go around in the latest training shoes and track suits. Their parents drive them to the Tennis Club or the Cricket Club. They cycle around on the latest mountain bikes and all seem to have the most expensive in-line skates that money could buy. I bet they've probably all got computers and games consoles as well. Frankly, they make me sick. But I must admit that I am jealous of them.

I tried to be friendly when I first arrived but they just ignored me. Mum explained to me that this was quite normal and things would get better with time. Weeks and then months passed with my situation becoming worse – not better. What was wrong with me? I was clean, I didn't smell and I wasn't looking for trouble.

Then it struck me one day what was wrong. It all came down to money. They had it and I didn't. In their eyes this fact, made me inferior to them. What could I do?

As I had only tatty old training shoes and old jeans, they laughed at me. Then one day, James Dixon from across the street said his Mum claimed that I "dressed like a beggar". This made them laugh and they began to shout, "beggar boy, beggar boy!" Now every time they see me I can hear them shouting, "beggar boy!"

It makes me mad!

"Tommy," mum shouted from the kitchen. "Would you go to the shops and get some milk for me please?"

Chapter 1

"Yes," I groaned in reply.

The last thing I wanted to do was go out on to the street and risk getting ridiculed by those wealthy idiots again. They always seemed to be hanging around with nothing better to do than annoy me. Their parents were just as bad. Despite not actually calling me names to my face, I could tell from the way they looked at me that they found my presence on their street disgusting.

"Here's some money to get yourself a treat," said Mum.

This cheered me up a little as I left the flat to head for the shops. At least we weren't so poor that we couldn't afford the odd treat now and then.

Chapter 2

"Won't be too long!" I shouted to Mum. I shut the door behind me and made my way up the steps to street level.

The garden flat is sunk below the level of the garden and the pavement. There is a wide path, which surrounds it, and inside it's not as dull as you would first expect. A set of steps brings you up to street level. Just as I approached the top of the steps I stopped and had a peek to see if anyone was in the street. I breathed a sigh of relief when I convinced myself the coast was clear.

Walking briskly along, I turned the corner into the street where the shops were. It was a bright sunny day and I was almost enjoying the journey. The gardens were in full bloom and the birds were chirping in the trees. Maybe it wasn't so bad here after all. It was certainly a lot better than the area we had moved from, although I sometimes wondered if I would have been happier there. At least where we had come from the people had little to boast about in terms of their wealth.

Everything seemed fine so far with none of my enemies in sight. The shop where I usually went to buy milk, groceries and newspapers was looming up ahead. It was quite a large shop – really more of a mini-market. Sitting outside were boxes of fruit and vegetables on display, which the shopkeeper was very proud of.

Chapter 2

I entered the shop to get the milk and some chocolate. The stout and bespectacled shopkeeper watched me closely as I looked around his shop. He was another person in the area who had no time for me.

"Yes, what do you want boy?" he said in a commanding tone of voice.

It was as though he had judged me on my appearance the very first time I entered his shop. That day he must have decided I had the appearance of a shoplifter and ever since then he has classed me as a thief without any reason. Although I knew I didn't look as smart as the other kids in this area, it didn't give him the right to automatically class me as a thief!

The shopkeeper continued, "If you're here to browse then leave. I only want people in my shop if they intend to buy goods!"

What a cheek! "I want some milk, actually," I stated.

"It's over there, in the corner," he replied.

I walked over and picked up some milk and then went to where the sweets were on display. As usual, confronted with a huge choice, I couldn't make my mind up what to buy. I also enjoyed the fact that the longer I spent in his shop, the more it annoyed him.

"Come on, you've got your milk," said the shopkeeper trying to rush me.

I grabbed the nearest chocolate bar and went to the till to pay for them. The shopkeeper didn't even say "thank you".

As I left the shop I thought I would annoy the shopkeeper even more. If he was going to continue being rude to me then I felt I was obliged to annoy him with my little remarks.

"Thank you very much for your courteous and friendly service. I must come back soon!" I said with a wide smile on my face.

The shopkeeper grimaced and I quickly stepped out of the shop.

Disaster! I bumped straight in into Rob Dixon and his brother Paul. They were about the same age as me but Rob was taller and Paul was of a broader build than I was. I knew from past experience, if it came to blows, that they would be the winners.

The brothers were what some would call "smooth". I thought of them as just plain "slimy". They both wore the latest track suits and gleaming white training shoes. Their hair was gelled back to make them look older and James had a diamond stud earring. They looked me up and down for a while as if I had no right to be breathing the same air as them.

Rob pushed me hard in the chest with

both hands. He then wiped his hands on his trousers as if to show by touching me he had made himself dirty.

"Been shoplifting then, beggar boy?" said Rob.

"It's what we expect from your sort," added his brother.

I didn't reply to their provocation.

"What's up? Too dumb to even speak?" continued Rob.

Paul then started on me with, "Look at the state of him! His type shouldn't be allowed to live here!"

"We used to dress like you until our Dad got a job!" mocked Paul.

"Oh, of course, you don't have a Dad, do you beggar boy!" added Rob as they both laughed.

Panicking, I tried to brush past them. As I did, Rob knocked the hand in which I was carrying the milk. The carton looped in the air and burst when it hit the street. The Dixon boys laughed at their mischief.

"That was for my Mum!" I cried.

Paul sneered and said, "Are you going to starve then beggar boy?"

The shopkeeper then appeared in the doorway.

"What are you boys up to?" he asked.

"He's dropped his milk. He's so clumsy," said Paul.

"He did pay for it didn't he?" remarked Rob in a tone of false concern towards the shopkeeper.

The shopkeeper nodded and asked me, "Do you want a replacement?"

"No!" I replied shaking my head. "I'll have to get some more money from my Mum."

A smirk appeared on the shopkeeper's face as he said, "That's just as well. I don't give credit to likes of you!"

I ran off down the street in a rage following that remark. Why were they all so horrible to me?

Chapter 3

As I ran into Montague Street I slowed up and started walking again. Calming down after my humiliation at the hands of the Dixon boys, I tried to convince myself that things weren't as bad as they seemed. My positive thinking was brought to an abrupt halt.

I jumped when a voice bellowed, "Have you been up to no good?"

It was one of my neighbours Major Jackson. He was a retired army officer with a reputation in the area for being very respectable, but also very grumpy. He had the kind of voice projection that made you jump to attention when he spoke. He stood there, six feet tall, with a very straight back, peering down at me. It was as if I was on parade and he was inspecting me. I could imagine that those who served under him were frightened to death of him.

"Me?" I asked in amazement.

"Don't be insolent boy! Why were you running then?" he questioned me.

I'd had enough and screamed, "I was just running and now I'm walking! Is that a crime in this area?"

I was staring directly at the Major's eyes when I said this, but he eyeballed me back with a very threatening glare. I averted my eyes from his and focused on his highly polished shoes instead.

The Major seemed very angry at my attitude towards him and he cried, "Don't raise your voice to me boy!"

Chapter 3

"I'm sorry," I immediately replied trying to defuse the situation. This old Major might think that it's still OK to thump boys like me about the head for no reason at all.

The Major continued, "I don't know what this area is coming to with your sort running wild around here. No wonder the crime rate is up!"

I stood there too frightened to move for a while.

"Be gone with you, and stay out of trouble!" ordered the Major.

With my head bowed I walked off slowly towards the flat. It just wasn't fair why was he picking on me?

The door creaked as I pushed it open. My Mum stood there in front of me.

"Where's the milk then?" she inquired.

I gulped and said, "Err, I sort of dropped it."

Mum let out a sigh and said, "Marvellous!"

She then looked at my hands and exclaimed, "But you still managed to get your chocolate!"

Nodding in embarrassment I offered, "I'll go back and get some more."

"Yes, we really need the milk, Tommy. Here's some money to get it," she said.

My heart knew that I had let my Mum down, but my head was telling me that I really didn't want to face those people who were so awful to me out there. She seemed to sense that something wasn't right.

She quizzed me, "Do you have a problem going to that particular shop?"

"Sort of," I replied in a sheepish tone. "It's the shopkeeper – we don't really see eye to eye – if you know what I mean."

Mum looked concerned and said, "You haven't been causing trouble there have you?"

I let out a loud sigh. Just as usual it must be my fault!

She got the message that I was disgusted with her remark and apologised, "Sorry."

"The shopkeeper thinks I'm only in his shop to steal things," I said.

My Mum replied, "Oh don't be silly Tommy – whatever gave you that impression?"

"It's the way he looks at me and talks to me," I explained.

She tried to console me and said, "Well if he does it again you better tell me about it and I'll sort him out."

Putting her arm around my shoulder and giving me hug she added, "And you try to be as polite as possible."

Chapter 4

Once again I checked to see if the coast was clear before venturing onto the street. Good! There was no sign of those Dixon boys or the grumpy old major. Maybe this time I could execute the simple task of going to the shop for milk without coming home empty handed, and sparking off World War III along the way.

As I stepped onto the street a sudden chill ran down my spine. I shuddered for a moment and then looked across the road. There stood a boy about my age. In fact, there stood a real scruffy looking boy. It amused me, for a moment, to think that there was a "real" beggar boy. If the neighbours could have a look at him, they maybe wouldn't give me such a hard time, I thought to myself. I knew it was wrong, but it even flashed through my head, "What's the likes of you doing here?"

The boy looked dirty. His red hair was cut very short and it looked so bad that he must have cut it himself. Could he be one of those New Age travellers? Dressed in an old hairy jumper and shabby torn jeans he looked a pathetic figure. On his feet were scruffy large boots, which had seen far better days. He wore that wounded expression of somebody who had been given a raw deal in life.

He sat there on the wall looking directly at me. Trying not to stare, I walked off down the street. Just as I was about to turn

Chapter 4

the corner, I looked back for a second glance. He was gone! Where did he go? There was no sign of him in the street, so he must have gone into a garden or something. I shrugged, and walked on wondering about his odd behaviour.

Then, out of the corner of my eye, I saw him across the street in front of me. Spooky! How did he manage to get there without passing me? Another shiver ran down my spine as our eyes met across the street. Why was he staring at me? Did he intend to rob or attack me? By this time I was frightened and hastily made my way to the shop.

"Ah, back again!" said the shopkeeper. "You should be more careful this time."

"But it was those other boys who knocked it out of my hand," I stated.

The shopkeeper shook his head and said, "There's no need to blame your clumsiness on other people."

"I'm not lying, it was their fault!" I pleaded.

The shopkeeper looked at me sternly and said, "I've known the Dixon boys for years, and they are good boys. Do you expect me to believe your version of events?"

I realised I was wasting my time with the man. He would never accept my word against their's. With my head bowed I paid for the milk and stepped out of the shop.

Still looking down at my feet I felt a sudden presence in front of me. I looked up, blinked, and received the fright of my life. There was the beggar boy right in front of me! We stared at each other for a while. This felt very uncomfortable for me, so I had to break the silence between us.

"What do you want? I don't have any money." I said.

The boy looked straight at me and said, "Don't be afraid, Tommy."

This is really weird, I thought. How could he possibly know my name? I'd never seen this boy until today. Up close, his face was dirty and his teeth were stained brown and rotten. His hands were grimy and had thick black lines of dirt under the fingernails. His clothes looked as though they hadn't been washed in months, and if they were washed, they would probably fall apart.

I questioned the boy, "How do you know my name?"

"That's not important, Tommy," he replied. "The people around here give you a hard time, don't they?"

This put me on the defensive and I said, "No, I get along just fine here."

The boy looked at me with sympathy and said, "I know what it feels like. I've been in your situation before."

"What do you know about my problems?" I asked.

The boy answered me, "I know the hurt, Tommy. I understand the humiliation."

Our conversation was broken, abruptly, by the shopkeeper.

"Who are you talking to out there?" he cried.

I turned to answer him and replied, "Just a boy."

"What boy?" said the shopkeeper.

He was gone! I looked up and down the street to find him. He surely couldn't have disappeared that quickly?

"The boy who was standing here a minute ago," I replied.

The shopkeeper was becoming angry and shouted, "Son, don't waste my time. Run off home now and talk to yourself there!"

"But I was talking to another boy just a

second ago!" I exclaimed.

Pointing up the street, the shopkeeper yelled, "Scram!"

There was no room for debate here and I ran off up the road. I stopped and turned around as I heard boxes crashing to the ground. Some of the shopkeeper's fruit and vegetable display in front of the shop had toppled over. A grin came to my face as I watched oranges and lettuces spilling out onto the road. The shopkeeper stood there scratching his head wondering how it had happened.

Could the boy have toppled the boxes as a prank?

Good grief! There was the beggar boy again. This time he was standing across the road from my house. I was about to cross the road to go and confront him when I heard a tapping from a window. Mrs Benson was waving a greeting to me.

After waving back and smiling for a second, I turned back around to go and talk to the boy. He was gone!

There was no sign of him in the street. I checked a few of the gardens, but there was no sign of him either. How could he make himself invisible so quickly? Maybe it was evidence of just how street-wise the boy was. I supposed that living rough like he does must sharpen the wits.

I was glad to enter the calm of my flat again. At least my mission had been accomplished this time. Milk had been purchased and delivered safely home.

Mum mockingly said, "Well done, I'll need to give you a gold star."

"Oh, no need," I replied. "I'll settle for the chocolate that I bought earlier."

Mum playfully swatted the top of my head and gave me the chocolate.

"Want a piece?" I said.

Chapter 5

The next morning, after breakfast, Mum decided what we were doing today. Mum would do the cleaning for Mrs Benson upstairs in the big house till lunchtime, and I was given the task of cleaning out a chest of drawers in our hallway. That suited me fine, as I didn't want to venture outside today with that mysterious boy lurking around.

"Mum, have you seen any strange boys hanging around here lately?" I coyly asked.

She replied, "Only one."

"Yes?" I continued in expectation.

"You!" said Mum laughing.

I scowled and said, "No, seriously – have you seen anyone strange around here in the past day or so?"

"What are you getting at Tommy?" asked Mum. "Has someone been annoying you?"

"Well no, not really," I replied. "It's just that I saw this strange beggar boy yesterday. He was hanging around here and he knew my name."

Mum frowned and said, "What would a beggar boy be doing around here?"

"That's what I thought!" I answered.

"Well, just stay away from him. I don't want you associating with any beggars," she said. "What would the neighbours think!"

With my position in the neighbourhood, I didn't think it would make much difference who I associated with. The neighbours might even have thought that I was bringing more poor people into the area just to annoy them. Knowing my luck that was probably just what they were thinking right.

How did the boy know my name though? He couldn't have heard it from the abuse I was getting because all they called me was "beggar boy". Maybe he heard Mum or Mrs Benson calling me? The thought that he knew my name and may have been spying on me worried and annoyed me.

Mum picked up Emma and said, "I'll be upstairs cleaning if you need anything."

"Fine," I said. "I'll get on with cleaning out those drawers."

The chest of drawers was quite tall, five drawers in total, with a dark mahogany finish. As far as I knew it was full of junk left by the previous occupant of the flat. I pulled open the top drawer and picked out bits of string, old electric plugs, shoe polish, pens and all manner of things. Working through the drawers, in descending order, I had amassed quite a pile of rubbish. Some of it was useful though, and being a bit of a hoarder, I would need to find somewhere to store the interesting stuff. As usual this probably involved a shoebox under my bed. One of my Mum's pet hates.

Finally, I opened the bottom drawer. To my surprise, it was empty apart from a page from an old newspaper. I was just about to close the door again when the hallway suddenly became icy cold. Then a blast of freezing wind blew the old newspaper page up out of the drawer and into the air. The page fluttered in the air for a moment and then landed in front of me.

I stood there motionless in surprise, as

Chapter 5

I couldn't understand where the wind had come from. The front door was shut and the other windows were barely open if at all. Coming to my senses again I looked carefully at the page at my feet. I gasped in amazement.

The headline read:

> "BEGGAR BOY KILLED
> IN MONTAGUE STREET"

I looked at the date. It was from 14th of May 1976. I read the story to discover that the boy who had been knocked down by a car was unknown. He was approximately thirteen years old, like me, and had been begging locally. Police also thought he might have been living rough in the area. It appeared that he had run out in front of a car in suspicious circumstances. The police thought the boy was being chased at the time, but no witnesses could confirm this.

The situation was really getting weird now. First there was the disappearing beggar boy, and now this news story had appeared before my eyes. What did it all mean?

I grabbed the page and ran up the stairs to where my Mum was cleaning.

"Look Mum," I cried.

I then babbled to her about the boy and the newspaper story. Maybe I was speaking too fast and didn't make any sense to her, but she didn't seem to listen to what I had been saying.

"Calm down Tommy!" she pleaded. "Are you feeling alright?"

"Yes Mum, I feel fine," I reassured her. "It's just such a spooky coincidence. Isn't it?"

Mum put her hand on my forehead to check my temperature and said, "Either that or a very active imagination!"

"I'm fine Mum honest!" I cried.

"You have been acting a bit strange lately Tommy. Are you sure there isn't anything bothering you?" she inquired again.

Mrs Benson then appeared in the room.

"What's all the commotion?" she asked.

My Mum looked embarrassed and answered, "Oh, it's just that Tommy has got something into his head about a beggar boy."

"Beggar boy?" Mrs Benson queried.

"Yes, here's a newspaper story I found in the drawers downstairs," I said.

Mrs Benson took the page from me and put on her reading glasses. She gave a nod of recognition as she read the story.

"A terrible tragedy," she pronounced. "It happened about twenty years ago just outside there in the street."

"What exactly happened?" asked my Mum.

Mrs Benson sighed and said, "It seemed a beggar boy was being chased and ran in front of a car. Killed him stone dead in an instant."

"That's terrible!" said my Mum.

"Yes it was," replied Mrs Benson. She continued: "The police had a suspicion that some local boys were involved in the incident, but nobody came forward to give any evidence."

"So nobody was ever brought to justice for causing the death of the boy," I announced.

"It seems that way," said Mrs Benson. "Anyway, I must be getting on, I'm meeting some friends for coffee at eleven o'clock."

"Did you know the boy at all?" I asked Mrs Benson as she was leaving the room.

"Oh, no!" she replied. "We didn't want to encourage his sort to stay around here."

Chapter 5

For a moment I was shocked by Mrs Benson's remark. She was just like the rest of the neighbours. Why couldn't they just be a little more tolerant?

Mum looked at me and said, "I've got work to do and so have you, Tommy."

I took my newspaper page and went back downstairs into the flat. As I cleared away the junk from the drawers I couldn't stop thinking about what happened to the beggar boy twenty years ago. Did he suffer the same torment as me, and was his the death the result?

It frightened me to think that I could easily end up being run over by a car, while being chased by my horrible neighbours. Was my meeting with the beggar boy yesterday just a coincidence?

Chapter 6

Mum came downstairs with Emma at noon to prepare the lunch for us all. She pulled a tin of spaghetti from the cupboard and waved it at me.

"Your favourite Tommy, spaghetti on toast!" she said with a smile. "It's your reward for cleaning out those drawers."

"Fine," I replied quietly.

In a few minutes we were sat at the kitchen table with the lunch before us. The spaghetti smelled great, but my appetite wasn't there. I had too much on my mind with the mysterious events of yesterday and today.

"Something wrong with the food?" Mum inquired.

"No, it's fine," I replied. "I'm just not very hungry."

I got up from the table and went to look out the kitchen window. This window looked out on to the steps that brought you up to the level of the garden. My attention turned to Emma for a second as she coughed. As I returned to gazing out of the window there he was.

"Look!" I cried.

The beggar boy was standing at the top of the steps looking down at me.

"Mum quick!" I pleaded turning to her.

Mum jumped out of her chair and raced to the window. She looked outside and sighed.

Chapter 6

"Tommy I've had enough of this non-sense!" she said.

I looked again at the top of the stairs and the boy was gone.

"He must have moved away when I called you," I explained.

"How convenient," Mum countered.

"I tell you he was there a second ago!" I cried.

Mum returned to her chair and sat down. I could tell she was not at all happy with me. She must have thought I was playing a cruel joke on her or possibly that I was going out of my mind. To be honest, I had been acting a bit odd lately, but I had good reason to be.

"Sit down by me, Tommy," ordered Mum. "You maybe saw a boy, but it's nothing to get all worked up about. If you carry on behaving like this I'll need to take you to a doctor."

I felt so confused now. I was certain I had seen the beggar boy, but I was ashamed that my behaviour was beginning to upset Mum. The only way that I could see to keep Mum and myself happy was to keep any future events on the subject to myself.

"I'm going out to get some fresh air," I said.

A puzzled look appeared on Mum's face.

"You haven't wanted to go outside for ages," she stated to me. "Why do you suddenly want to go out now?"

I shrugged my shoulders and replied, "I just want to, that's all."

"You worry me," said Mum as I made for the door.

"Won't be long!" I shouted as I raced up the steps to ground level.

Instead of checking to see if my enemies

were out of sight, I boldly strode onto the pavement. There was only one thing on my mind, and that was to confront this beggar boy.

I knew it! There was the beggar boy walking down the street away from me.

I plucked up all my courage and yelled, "Hey you! I want to talk to you!"

The boy continued walking without acknowledging by cries. He turned the corner into the street where the shop was. I decided I must confront the boy and started running after him. As I turned the corner I came to a halt. He was gone! How did he manage to keep evading me so easily? My eyes screwed up as I peered down the street looking for any sign of him. After a minute I gave up and felt downhearted. Maybe I was seeing things after all?

I turned to go back home, and as I did I

nearly jumped out of my skin! There right in front of me was the beggar boy.

"You almost gave me a heart attack!" I cried. "What's the meaning of sneaking up behind me like that?"

"Don't be alarmed Tommy," said the boy, "I'm here to help you."

Chapter 7

As I tried to wonder what the beggar boy meant by "help", I suddenly heard a rush of footsteps. It was the Andrews gang! Before I knew it they had surrounded me and were chanting gleefully, "beggar boy! beggar boy!"

The Andrews family lived a couple of houses up the street from us. The parents were both directors of some city firm and they completely spoiled their kids. Anything that the three brothers and one sister wanted they got. It was hard to judge which family were the most horrible – the Andrews or the Dixons. In the end I called it a dead heat.

The eldest of the Andrews, Thomas, who was fifteen, pushed me against a wall. His two younger brothers and his sister took this as a cue to do the same. They all stood there sneering at me.

"When are you going to take the message and get lost!" Thomas shouted into my face.

"Leave me alone!" I cried, "I've done nothing to you!"

Alex Andrews, who was only nine, held his nose and said, "But we can smell you from streets away!"

"Yes, you belong on a farm – not here," chimed his sister, Charlotte, as she held her nose as well.

In a way I felt sorry for the younger members of the Andrews family. With older brothers like Thomas and Nigel setting the example, what chance did Alex and Charlotte have? It was only natural for them to copy their older brothers and grow up into horrid little human beings.

It was then I realised the beggar boy had disappeared again. What a big help he had turned out to be! He offers to help me and when the trouble appears he's off in a flash.

"Go and run off home to Mummy!" shouted Nigel, the other brother.

They let me past, and as I was about run away I felt Thomas's boot on my backside. I yelped with the pain and ran as fast as I could.

I could hear them shouting, "Smelly beggar boy! Smelly beggar boy!"

As I turned back into Montague Street there was the beggar boy in front of me again. Rage filled my mind and I was ready to vent some of it on this "real" beggar boy.

"Where did you get to?" I asked abruptly as my nostrils flared.

"I was around," was his casual reply.

He didn't seem at all troubled by my obvious anger directed at him. Was he just acting "cool", or did he really not care?

"You said you could help me!" I continued.

"All you have to do is ask," he replied calmly.

"Yes, I want help!" I cried. "The people around here are horrible to me!"

The boy then remarked, "They were to me as well."

What did he mean by saying that? Maybe he had been begging around here before I arrived in the neighbourhood, and had suffered at the hands of these awful kids.

"Do you mean the Andrews and Dixons

gave you a rough time as well?" I asked in a more reasonable tone.

"Not them, but others have made life difficult," he answered.

I was puzzled by his response and queried, "What others?"

"You wouldn't know them. The people have changed around here, but their attitudes haven't," he replied.

Eager to learn more about the boy I asked, "So you had the same trouble as me a while ago?"

"Yes, that's one way of putting it," said the boy in an almost humorous tone of voice.

Why did he find the situation of being bullied and intimidated faintly funny? I began to wonder if he knew anything about the events of twenty years ago. After clearing my throat I decided to quiz the boy about the events of the past.

"Do you know anything about the boy who was knocked down and killed here twenty years ago?" I asked.

The boy looked away and gave me no answer. His refusal to answer made me press him further.

I continued, "There was a boy like you killed here – do you know the facts?"

"We both know what happened," answered the boy clearly indicating that he did not want to discuss the subject any further.

Why should he seem so awkward about discussing what happened twenty years ago? Could it possibly be that the dead boy was his brother or another relative? Anyway I thought I'd better not press him too hard on the subject for the present. He was, after all, my new ally in my battles with the ignorant people around here.

Chapter 7

I changed the subject to the present day and my problems.

"How can you help me then?" I asked the boy.

His eyes lit up at my question and he replied, "I have my methods."

The answer was once again just too cryptic for my liking. I had to find out what he really was meaning.

"What do you mean 'methods'?" I said.

The boy smiled and replied, "You'll see – I'm sure the results will meet with your satisfaction!"

"Good, who shall we visit first?" I inquired.

He rubbed his chin in deep thought.

"Let's start with the Andrews'."

I clasped my hands together with the excitement of the thought of a little revenge and said, "When can we start?"

"I think tonight will do nicely!" was his

prompt reply. "I'll come and get you when I'm ready. Don't let your Mum know anything about this!"

"Yes, anything you say," I replied.

"Now go back home and act normal until I come for you tonight," ordered the boy.

Nodding my head in agreement, I set off back to the flat. As I walked along I realised that I didn't even know the boy's name. I'd have to find that out the next time I saw him.

"Hi Mum!" I cried as I breezed through the door still in a state of excitement.

"That walk seems to have cheered you up. Did you find the mysterious vanishing beggar boy then?" Mum smiled.

I thought for a moment and then replied, "No, not really."

Although I hated lying to my Mum like this, it seemed the only course of action at

Chapter 7

the moment. Besides she thought the whole beggar boy story was just down to my vivid imagination.

Chapter 8

Once again my appetite failed me at dinner. The excitement at the impending adventure tonight had blunted any hunger I felt. This met with great disapproval from Mum. She hated food being wasted – especially on our tight budget.

"What's the point in me preparing good food if it's only going to go to waste?" she asked.

"I just don't feel hungry just now." I said.

Mum was obviously getting concerned

about my health and followed, "If your appetite doesn't return to normal soon, it's off to the doctors with you my lad!"

I sometimes wondered if my Mum knew the extent of the misery that I was going through with the neighbours. At times she did seem very concerned about me, but at others she appeared to blame it on me being over-sensitive. With Emma only being a baby though, I guess she must have had more important things to worry about.

After watching some TV, I faked a huge yawn and stated, "I think I'll go to bed now."

Looking at me, with more than a hint of suspicion, she said, "OK, sleep tight."

I climbed into bed with my clothes on and shuffled under the covers. That way if Mum came in to check on me she would think I was in my pyjamas.

Chapter 8

Reaching under the bed I pulled out a shoebox. Inside the box was the junk I had saved from cleaning out the drawers. Neatly folded on top was the yellowed newspaper page containing the headline about the beggar boy. I read it over and over again trying to get any indication of what the boy was actually like. It was a pity the description of him was very vague, and they did not even have a name or a photograph of him. For some reason I just imagined that he was exactly like the boy I had met.

As I lay in my bed I wondered what plans for tonight the beggar boy had? Would he even turn up at all? I recalled the incident at the shop with the fruit display with glee. I couldn't know for sure that the mess was his doing, but I had a pretty fair idea that it was down to him. Maybe practical jokes were his style? But what if he had something more nasty planned? Being a bit of a coward this struck a chord of fear with me. It could be that he could make matters even worse for me! If Mum found out I'd been up to no good, especially with a beggar boy, it would be curtains for me.

Time passed so slowly – the anticipation was killing me! When would the beggar boy come and call me?

Chapter 9

There was a tap at the window. I awoke suddenly and nearly jumped out of bed. I must have been dozing. The clock read ten minutes to midnight. There at the window was the pale sad face of the beggar boy. He beckoned me to come with him. Opening the window, I quietly slipped out into the night air with the beggar boy.

"Just stand behind the hedge there and watch what happens," he ordered.

"What are you going to do?" I asked.

The boy turned to me with a wide grin

and said, "Give them a little fright – that's all."

I watched as the boy crossed the road and disappeared around the back of the Andrews' house. The house stood in complete darkness. What was the boy going to do?

Squinting to see my watch in the darkness, I figured he'd been gone at least five minutes. Maybe he'd been frightened off by someone? Even worse – could he be playing a big practical joke on me?

Then I saw a light come on in one of the rooms. After a minute it went off again. Another light went on in another room immediately. This was followed by lights going on and off in all the rooms seemingly at random.

Suddenly there was a blood-curdling shriek from the Andrews' house. I could see frightening and threatening looking shadows in the rooms where the lights were on. There were more screams from the house. What on earth was the boy doing in there?

I was startled as a window blew out and the curtains flapped as if in a fierce wind, although the night air was quite still. How could that happen? The lights still continued to flash on and off and the screams continued. I was shocked by what the boy was doing but I was also mightily impressed! That would teach those Andrews a lesson they wouldn't forget.

The front door of the house then flew open and nearly came off its hinges. The sound of demonic laughter echoed from the house and into the night. Out rushed the Andrews, falling over each other in a mad scramble to escape. They were completely panic-stricken and wailing at each other as they ran down the street in their pyjamas. I stifled a laugh as I watched them run around the corner and into the night.

I then looked back at the Andrews' house. It was now silent and in total darkness. Where there had been mayhem a second ago was now a scene of complete stillness. There was no sign of the boy though. I couldn't wait to congratulate him on what a great job he had done. I had no idea what he had planned to do, but the events I'd just witnessed were beyond my wildest dreams!

The night air began to feel cold and I wondered where the boy had gone. I stayed behind the hedge for a few minutes and then decided to go over to the Andrews' house and try to find him.

I reached the open front door and said quietly, "Are you there?"

Not a sound!

Chapter 9

"Come on stop fooling!" I continued. "That was great! How do you do it?"

There was no sign of the boy. He must have left the house and gone to his home – wherever that was. That was a shame because I was desperate to thank him for his efforts and to find out more about his tricks.

Checking to see nobody was around, I quickly crossed the street and down the steps to my bedroom window. Climbing back through the window I slipped and fell in a heap on the floor. Mum must have heard me! I could hear footsteps.

Without a second to spare I had changed into my pyjamas. The door swung open and Mum stood there.

"Tommy, what are you doing?" she whispered angrily.

I had to think fast and said, "I was just opening the window – it was so stuffy in here."

Mum eyed me suspiciously and then looked at the window. She must have been convinced by my explanation.

"Next time open it more quietly because you could wake up Emma. Goodnight!" she said as she left me and returned to her own bedroom.

Breathing easily once again, I climbed into my own bed and drifted off to sleep with a contented feeling. That was the Andrews sorted out!

Chapter 10

The following morning was uneventful when compared to the antics of last night. I was bursting to tell somebody about the routing of the Andrews, but the only person I could safely talk to now was the beggar boy. And where was he?

Mum appeared from upstairs after talking to Mrs Benson for a long while. She seemed excited as she entered the kitchen.

"What's up?" I asked knowingly.

She took a deep breath and replied, "You will never guess what happened last night?"

"What?" I asked trying my best to stifle a wicked grin.

Mum continued, "Well, it seems the Andrews were haunted out of their house last night."

"Haunted?" I prompted, waiting for more details.

"Yes, they were frightened out of their wits. They ran off to the cathedral a few streets away and have refused to leave there ever since!" she answered.

By this time I couldn't hide the huge grin on my face.

Mum reacted swiftly to this and cried, "Tommy, it's no laughing matter!"

I cleared my throat and put on a straight face.

"Any more details?" I said.

Mum sat down and said, "Apparently all the lights started flashing and then there were horrible screams like banshees."

"Go on," I encouraged her.

"The Andrews said terrifying ghostly figures appeared and chased them out of the house," said Mum with a concerned look on her face.

I pushed my luck and inquired further, "Anything else?"

Disapproving of my morbid interest she paused for a moment and continued, "They said words appeared on the walls which seemed to be written with blood."

A shiver ran up my spine at this detail and I wriggled in revulsion. The beggar boy really had delivered the works! Sure, I wanted revenge on the Andrews but maybe he had gone a bit too far.

"What did the words say?" I asked.

Mum thought for a while, trying to recall the story as Mrs Benson must have told it to her.

"Leave Us in Peace!" said Mum with a

puzzled look on her face. "What do you think that means Tommy?"

I shrugged my shoulders and replied, "I don't know."

Of course this phrase made perfect sense to me. It was just the beggar boy fooling around and warning them off. He really had done a complete number on them.

Mum then said something that made me tense up immediately.

"Maybe it's got something to do with your mysterious beggar boy?" she announced.

I couldn't tell if Mum was joking or not, but I gave her a brief dumb smile.

She then hit me with another stunner.

"Shops, Tommy?" she asked.

I sighed and replied, "OK Mum."

At least the Andrews were out of the way now, so there was less of a chance of being hassled.

Chapter 10

With some money in my pocket I trudged up the steps and on to the street. Vainly, I looked around for a sight of the boy. As usual when you wanted to see him he wasn't there. I was walking along the street where the shops were when a voice from behind made me jump.

"Tommy!" said the voice.

I recognised it instantly – it was the voice of the beggar boy.

Smiling with admiration I asked, "Where did you get to last night?"

"My job was done," answered the boy calmly.

"And what a job that was – well done!" I exclaimed. "How did you manage to do all those things last night?"

"As I explained, I have my methods," he replied.

Impatiently I questioned him again, "Yes alright – but what are your tricks?"

The boy shook his head and said, "I can't ever reveal them to you."

This answer annoyed me and I pleaded, "Oh come on! We're in this together."

"No!" said the boy in a voice which made it very clear he did want to discuss the matter any further.

We walked slowly towards the shop and I asked him, "You will still help me get revenge on the others, won't you?"

With a smile the boy replied, "Yes of course. Shall we see what we can do with the Major and the shopkeeper – they've been rotten to you haven't they?"

"Sounds good to me!" I gleefully replied.

On reaching the shop I walked in first. I was intent in proving to the shopkeeper that I had not been talking to myself outside of his shop the other day, as he had claimed.

"See? Here's the boy I was talking to!" I said as I caught the attention of the shop-keeper.

The shopkeeper laughed and said, "You have a real problem boy!"

I looked behind me and the boy had disappeared yet again. What was his problem?

The shopkeepers tone became more sinister as he said, "Don't waste my time. Buy whatever you need and get out of my shop!"

Feeling very foolish, I quickly grabbed what Mum had told me to buy. The shop-keeper slammed my change on the counter and pointed to the door with a very stern look upon his face.

As I reached the door I said, "You'll see, I wasn't kidding you!"

"Out!" shouted the shopkeeper.

As I looked around outside I couldn't

see the boy anywhere. He certainly was an expert at making himself scarce. Why did he keep disappearing when other people were around?

Walking back to the flat I half expected the beggar boy to appear. Once again he seemed to appear out of nowhere.

"Did he give you a hard time again?" said the boy's voice from behind me.

I turned around to face him and cried, "Will you stop sneaking up behind me – it gives me the creeps the way you do that!"

The beggar boy ignored me and said, "Well, did he?"

"Yes, he did," I replied.

"We'll need to settle our account with him then, won't we?" stated the boy.

"Yes!" I said, and posed the boy a question. "But can you tell me why you keep dodging out of sight whenever other people are about?"

Chapter 10

"It's just my way," was his response.

Unsatisfied I continued, "I'm being made to look a fool because of you."

The boy looked puzzled and said, "How so?"

"Every time I try to show you to somebody, you dive out of the way," I answered.

There was no explanation given by the boy as to his odd behaviour as we walked on. He just didn't want to talk about how he slipped in and out of view.

In the distance I could see the Major polishing his car. Gleaming in the sunlight, the Major's car was his pride and joy. I bet he was waiting to have a go at me as well.

"Look, there's the Major," I pointed out to the boy.

The boy spied him in the distance and said, "Will he give you a hard time as well?"

"Probably," I replied.

The boy appeared deep in thought for a while and then announced, "I know – we can kill two birds with the one stone!"

I didn't understand and said meekly, "What do you mean?"

He grinned and said, "I'm sure I know of a way to get them at each other's throats."

"Who?" I said.

"The Major and the shopkeeper you fool!" he impatiently answered.

A light clicked on in my mind. The beggar boy had plans for revenge involving the Major and the shopkeeper at the same time. Now that should be interesting!

"I've got to go now," said the boy. "I'll come and get you before the fun begins!"

Now my attention turned to the Major who was looming up ahead. I wished I could make myself invisible as I approached him.

Chapter 10

He seemed to be ignoring me, but just as I was almost past him he remarked:

"Up to no good I expect! Do you know anything about that nonsense last night, boy?" he interrogated.

Feeling awkward I quickly replied, "No sir!"

"Are you sure?" he questioned me further.

I panicked and said, "No, I've got to get back. My Mum will be wondering where I am."

As I walked quickly away I heard the Major say: "Good! I'm glad your Mother cares about what you are up to. Young scallywags like you shouldn't be roaming the streets and annoying decent folks like us."

What a cheek! However, I didn't stay annoyed for long as my mind filled with the thought of what the beggar boy had in store for him. I would look forward to that day.

Chapter 11

It was quite early the very next morning. There was a rap at my bedroom window. I rubbed my eyes and fell out of bed to see who it was. As I opened the curtains the bright sunlight strained my eyes, but there I could see the beggar boy standing at the other side of the window.

I opened the window as quietly as I could because I did not want to waken Emma or my Mum.

"What is it? It's seven thirty you know," I said quietly.

"The Major's going to the shop – this is our chance!" he replied.

"Shh! Keep it down or you'll wake my Mum." I implored him.

The boy beckoned me to come with him. Dressing as fast as I could, I was soon clambering through the window and out into the early morning air.

"The Major's going for his usual morning paper. I'll follow him in and cause some mayhem between them," explained the boy.

"Can I watch?" I asked.

"Of course, they'll be too busy fighting one another to notice you," he said.

We caught sight of the Major walking along the street and followed behind at a safe distance. There wasn't a soul in the streets apart from us. Early each morning he always went for his newspaper and a few small items such as milk or pipe tobacco. Being a very respected customer I couldn't imagine how the boy was going to cause trouble between them.

As the Major entered the shop we ran to catch him up. Edging up to the shop window we peered in. There were the Major and the shopkeeper having a polite conversation.

"Right, I'll sneak in and have some fun!" said the beggar boy.

"Be careful," I pleaded.

I watched as the boy sneaked into the shop unnoticed. He hid himself behind a display of magazines. The Major then went to find something he wanted in the shop. While he was browsing for what he wished, I saw the boy come up behind him and delicately place a huge chocolate bar in the outside pocket of his jacket. It sat there – the silver foil wrapping gleaming like a beacon. To my amazement the Major didn't notice a thing!

The shopkeeper stood at his till and was adding up the price of the Major's purchases. At first he didn't seem to take any notice. Only when the Major was about to leave the shop did he notice the chocolate bar.

He shouted, "Wait a minute!"

The Major turned to look at the shopkeeper and said, "Is there a problem my good man?"

Staring at the Major's pocket he pointed to the chocolate bar and said, "What's that?"

The Major looked confused and said, "What are you on about?"

"That chocolate in your pocket!" accused the shopkeeper.

The major looked at the contents of his pocket in disbelief, and exclaimed, "How did that get there?"

"Obviously you must have put it there," said the shopkeeper sternly.

Chapter 11

The Major took great offence at the remark and replied, "Well I never! What a damned cheek you have."

Raising his voice the shopkeeper said, "You were going to steal that chocolate, weren't you?"

"How dare you – I don't know how it got there!" shouted the Major in reply.

"I've been losing a lot of stock lately, but I would never have dreamt it was you!" cried the shopkeeper.

Looking aghast at the accusation the Major bellowed, "You accuse me of stealing? I don't have to stand here and listen to this!"

As the Major tried to make his exit, the shopkeeper lunged over the counter and grabbed him.

"No you don't!" yelled the shopkeeper.

The Major wrestled with his captor and screamed, "Unhand me you fool!"

As the pair struggled in the shop, the beggar boy inflamed the situation by knocking over shelves of goods and throwing other things into the air. There were also screams and insults, which did not come from the mouths of either the Major or the shopkeeper, but from the beggar boy.

"You old thief – I knew it was you all along!" yelped a voice like the shopkeepers, but it didn't seem to come from him.

Similarly, a voice meant to be the Majors threatened, "I'll get you for this you impudent fool."

I supposed the Major and the shopkeeper must have been too busy fighting to notice there was another person in the shop impersonating their voices and making matters worse.

Suddenly I spied another man in the street. He came towards me and looked into the shop.

Chapter 11

"What's all that about – is it a robbery?" he inquired.

"I don't know," I replied.

By this time the pair of them were on the floor rolling around in a mess of milk, sugar, flour, eggs and shredded newspapers. There seemed to be a whirlwind in the shop blowing around them creating a scene like a fight in a cartoon. I laughed to see them making such fools of themselves.

The man looked at me with a frown and said, "I'd better put a stop to this!"

He went inside and separated the battling pair who were still trading insults.

Holding them apart he said, "Come to your senses gentlemen!"

It seemed as though both the Major and the shopkeeper knew the man who had separated them.

"Thank goodness it's you Mr Jones!" said the Major.

Wiping a mass of sugar and milk, amongst other things, from his face the shopkeeper said, "Arrest that man – he's been shoplifting!"

"He assaulted me, Mr Jones," pleaded the Major.

Trying to calm the situation, Mr Jones remarked, "Will you take a look at yourselves?"

The pair of them must have suddenly realised how foolish they must look. A retired and respected Major caught shoplifting, and a shopkeeper who attacked him. Both of them would be humiliated by the events of this morning. Their reputations would now be in ruins. Great!

But where had the beggar boy gone? He wasn't in the shop anymore, and he hadn't left through the front door. While Mr Jones was calming the incident down, the boy must have seized his chance and sneaked out the back door.

Chapter 11

I slipped quietly away from the scene with a satisfied grin on my face. I wondered how the beggar boy had managed to remain unseen in the shop and then make his escape? It seemed the boy had a wonderful trick of making himself invisible. There was no other way that I could think of to explain how he could escape from that shop undetected.

Climbing back through the window I heard footsteps. The door burst open and there stood Mum with Emma in her arms.

She couldn't believe her eyes and said, "What are you doing up and dressed at this time?"

"I thought I would go for a newspaper for you to read over breakfast," I replied with a straight face.

Mum gave me a strange look and then said, "What are you up to?"

"I'm just trying to make up for my odd

behaviour lately," I quickly replied in the hope that this response would get me off the hook.

Mum turned away and said, "Very well – off you go."

Chapter 12

When I reached the shop again it had a sign on the door saying:
"CLOSED UNTIL FURTHER NOTICE."

There was a small crowd of would-be customers loitering in the street. Apart from being annoyed at the inconvenience of the shop being closed, they were all having a good gossip about the bust-up between the Major and the shopkeeper. Opinions seemed to split evenly as to whether the Major or the shopkeeper was to blame, or the pair of them equally.

While some people defended the Major because he was retired and may have been becoming absent-minded, others took the opportunity to blacken his name because he was so grumpy most of the time. The shopkeeper did not escape criticism either. His surly and abrupt nature was claimed to be the cause of the furore. It gladdened my heart to hear that both of their reputations had been ruined in this neighbourhood.

On returning to the flat without a newspaper for Mum she remarked, "What now?"

"The shop was shut," I replied innocently.

I could have gone on to explain the circumstances of the closure to Mum, but I thought it better if I just acted ignorant. That way I would not bring any suspicion onto myself. If Mum had the slightest no-tion that I was involved with the beggar boy she would go nuts.

Mum was upstairs with Emma all morning, cleaning for Mrs Benson. To pass the morning I pretended to be reading comics, but in reality I was reliving every moment of the chaos in the shop. Anyone, to look at me, would think I was mad, as I laughed uncontrollably out loud from time to time.

As lunchtime approached I heard Mum's footsteps coming down the stairs. She looked excited when she entered the room, and I had a good idea why. However I didn't want to give my secret away, so I didn't say a word and waited until she had settled Emma down.

"More revelations!" exclaimed Mum.

Trying to seem disinterested as I looked up from my comic I murmured, "What?"

Mum continued, "You know why the shop was closed this morning?"

I nodded trying to keep my face from breaking into a smile.

"Mrs Benson was on the phone to one of her friends, and it seems that old Major and the shopkeeper had a fight in the middle of the shop. Can you believe that?" cried Mum.

I felt it was safe to grin a little, and enquired, "What were they fighting over?"

Mum eagerly replied, "It seems rather confused, but some say that the Major was caught stealing, and some say that the shopkeeper attacked him for no reason at all."

"That's terrible!" I added in mock surprise.

"They had to be separated by a passerby and the shop was left in a real mess as well," explained Mum.

"Well Mum, it goes to show that the people around here may not be as respect-

Chapter 12

able as they like to think they are," I remarked.

"You could be right there, Tommy!" said Mum. "Mrs Benson and the other neighbours will be talking about this for ages."

We both laughed for a while but stopped when the doorbell rang. Mum went to see who was there and I listened from the kitchen.

A deep voice said, "Sorry to disturb you madam I'm from the local police."

"What can I help you with?" said Mum.

The policeman continued, "You may have heard about an incident in the local shop this morning."

My heart raced as I wondered why the policeman had called here at my flat.

Mum replied, "Yes I heard about it from Mrs Benson who lives upstairs."

"Well it appears a young boy may have

been a witness to the events in the shop between the Major and the shopkeeper," explained the policeman.

Oh no! The man who broke up the fight in the shop must have told the police that he had spoken to a boy. The police were now making enquiries with all the boys in the local area.

"My Tommy was in bed," said Mum. "He's usually a late riser."

The policeman seemed satisfied and said, "Well thank you for your time madam, we just have to make sure."

I thought I was off the hook when suddenly Mum called me to her side, "Tommy come here!"

Quaking with fear I approached the door where the policeman stood.

"You were in bed until about nine, weren't you Tommy?" Mum asked.

"Yes," I replied in a feeble voice.

Smiling, the policeman said, "You certainly match the description, Tommy, but you can't be two places at once."

I felt a great weight roll off my shoulders when the policeman said this. What a relief!

"Good day," said the policeman as he turned and made his way up the steps.

Mum closed the door and we both walked back through to the kitchen.

Mum said, "Maybe it was that beggar boy, you claim to have seen, who was outside the shop?"

"Could be," I answered trying to hide my guilt.

Although the beggar boy was helping me get revenge on those who had humiliated me in the past, I found myself telling more lies to my Mum. It was a situation I didn't like. Mum had brought me up to always tell the truth.

Chapter 13

A few days had passed since the incident in the shop between the Major and the shopkeeper. Mum had mentioned a few times that it was all the neighbours were talking about. The Major hadn't been seen for days and rumour had it that he felt so embarrassed that he was going to move away from the area. I decided to go the shop and see what the situation was there.

It was another fine day as I walked along the street. I felt a lot happier about going out now because most of the people who used to torment me had left the area thanks to the beggar boy. Although I kept a look out for him each day, I hadn't seen the boy since his escape from the back of the shop. I wondered if he had left the area to lie low for a while?

On walking towards the shop I noticed a big red "FOR SALE" sign in the window. The shopkeeper must have felt so embarrassed by his actions the other day that he had decided to sell up.

It was rumoured around the neighbourhood that many of his customers would never shop there again after his trouble with the Major. They believed that even if the Major had mistakenly tried to leave without paying for something, then the shopkeeper could have handled the situation without violence.

As I peered through the shop window I felt a presence behind me. I knew immediately who it was.

Chapter 13

"Not bad for a morning's work!" said the beggar boy.

"Great," I replied. "Where have you been?"

The boy smiled and said, "Oh, here and there."

"How did you manage to remain unseen in the shop – and manage to escape as well?" I questioned him.

He shrugged his shoulders and replied, "I've told you – I have my methods."

"Who does that leave now to sort out?" he asked me.

I rubbed my chin and said, "Only the Dixons I suppose."

"I wonder what we can do with them?" said the boy.

He turned away from me and began walking up the street.

I was curious and asked, "Where are you off to now?"

"Follow me!" ordered the boy.

Following behind him I saw that we were fast approaching the Dixons' house. The boy stopped and we stood outside for a while. A figure appeared at one of the windows for a second. Did that person see us? I didn't think it was a wise idea for us to stick around like sitting ducks.

I said, "Come on let's go before they come out."

"Stay there," ordered the boy.

He set off towards the Dixon's front door.

"What are you going to do?" I cried.

Without replying the boy strode up to the front door and pressed the doorbell. He pressed it again and again and again. The Dixons would go mad if they saw either of us. I ducked behind a wall for a second and then peered over to see what was happening. The boy had gone. He must have been hiding when suddenly the door opened. It was Paul Dixon. He looked around for a while and then slammed the door shut.

A few seconds later the boy was back again ringing the doorbell. They must catch him this time I thought. I blinked and the boy was out of site again. Paul Dixon answered the door again and looked around. He came out into his garden for a further look for his mysterious caller.

"No sign of anyone!" yelled Paul to his brother who was now standing in the doorway.

The pair went back inside their house and the boy appeared again at the door. He rang the doorbell again. He's gone too far this time, I thought, the Dixon brothers would be waiting for him.

The door flew open and the Dixons charged out.

"Where are you?" yelled Paul. But the boy had disappeared again.

His brother chimed in, "Don't try to make a fool out of us – we'll get you!"

I was about to retreat to the safety of my flat when the beggar boy's voice cried from behind me, "Over here you chumps!"

Frozen with fear I looked at the beggar boy. Why had he dropped us right in it with the Dixons?

They were running towards us quickly when the boy said, "Follow me."

I ran for my life as I heard them shouting, "We'll get you beggar boy!"

We ran along the pavement to the end of the street with the Dixons close behind us. The beggar boy then veered onto the road.

"Come on!" he encouraged me.

I didn't stop to look or think and followed him. Suddenly I saw a car, very close, out of the corner of my eye.

Chapter 13

Time seemed to go into slow motion. I thought the car couldn't possibly miss me. I'm going to die! There was a tremendous screech of brakes. Then I felt a heavy push in my back. It must have been the beggar boy throwing me out of the way of the car. I landed in a heap at the side of the pavement and turned around to see the car plough into the beggar boy. In disbelief I closed my eyes and wished for it all to be a dream.

As I opened my eyes a second later I could see that the car was, in fact, a police car. The two officers jumped out of the car immediately. One came over to check on me and the other went over to apprehend the Dixon brothers.

"Are you alright son?" said the policeman. "That was a close one – did those other boys chase you onto the road?"

Badly shaken I pointed to the police car and said, "What about the boy?"

The policeman appeared puzzled and replied, "What boy?"

I explained to him, "The boy who pushed me out of the way just in time – you must have hit him!"

"You were the only boy in the road," said the officer.

Feeling distraught I cried, "You must have hit him, he had no chance!"

The officer looked around to his car to reassure himself and said, "Look for yourself there was nobody else involved."

"But there was – he saved my life!" I explained.

The officer looked at me sympathetically and said, "I think you've had a bump on the head son. Lay quietly there till we make sure you are alright."

After a few moments I sat up and looked over to where I had almost my death. There were long skid marks up to where the police car now sat in the middle of the road.

"I'm fine," I said as I got to my feet.

The boy was nowhere to be seen!

A few yards away the other officer was still cautioning the Dixon boys. Both of their faces were drained with shock and Paul was shaking. This episode had frightened the life out of them and being in trouble with the police was sure to bring stiff punishment from their embarrassed parents.

I shouted to them, "Where did the boy go?"

They looked at me strangely and replied in unison, "What boy? We were chasing after you."

My confusion was broken by my Mum's cries of, "Tommy! Tommy!"

Embracing me with a huge hug she explained that Mrs Benson had seen it all and came down to inform her.

Mrs Benson appeared a few moments later and said, "Are you alright Tommy?"

I sighed and replied, "Yes – but did you see what happened to the other boy?

"Other boy?" queried Mrs Benson. "I only saw you being chased by those Dixon boys. I hope they get what they deserve."

Looking around the street a final time, before being led away by Mum, I could only wonder what happened to the boy? I never even knew his name.

"We'll be in touch shortly," said one of the policemen.

Chapter 14

I lay in bed that night but couldn't sleep. Where had the boy gone and why had nobody seen him at the scene of the accident? It seemed to me that he had almost staged the whole thing. After all, it was him who goaded the Dixons into chasing after us. By running across the road like that he must have known that I was bound to follow him without thinking about my own safety.

It was incredible to think that he could

have planned to have the Dixons chase me onto the road just as a police car was coming along. All that to get the Dixons into trouble with the police? He had really gone too far this time. Or did the facts really add up? I couldn't be imagining the beggar boy could I?

Drifting off to sleep, I was startled by a rap at the window. It must be him! I drew back the curtains and there he was on the other side of the window. A mixture of relief and joy filled my heart. He wasn't dead and he couldn't be a figment of my imagination. Eagerly I opened the window to talk to the boy who had saved my life.

"Thank goodness you're alright," I cried.

"Yes, I'm fine," replied the boy very calmly.

I asked him, "Where did you get to then?"

The boy thought for a moment and then answered, "When I saw the police were involved I thought I'd better make myself scarce."

His explanation seemed plausible enough to me, as I was so happy to see him again. This boy has pushed me out of the way of a car at great danger to himself. He was my saviour.

"You must meet my Mum, she would love to thank you," I said.

"No, I don't think so," he replied sternly.

I tried to reason with him, "Oh come on – it's only my Mum!"

"I'm going away now Tommy," he said.

Taken aback by his statement I protested, "But you can't!"

"My work here is done," announced the boy.

He turned and marched up the steps

and away. How could he leave so suddenly without me having the chance to thank him properly? I didn't even get to know his name.

I heard footsteps and then my bedroom door swung open. It was Mum. She must have heard me opening the window and talking to the boy.

She looked concerned and said, "What are you up to?"

"It was the beggar boy – he was here a second ago!" I cried.

Coming over to the window she looked out into the darkness. I could tell from her face that she did not believe me.

"There's nobody there," she said.

I nodded and added, "I know – he said he was leaving."

"You claim he's saved your life and now he doesn't want to hang around for any thanks?" said Mum.

Chapter 14

"He said his work here was done," I answered.

Putting the palm of her hand on my brow, she felt to see if I was running a temperature. The window was shut and the curtains drawn closed again.

Leading me back to bed she said, "We'd better see a doctor in the morning. I think you've had a bit of a shock."

Knowing it was useless to try and convince her of his existence, I curled up and tried to get some sleep.

Morning came and I rose out of bed with a feeling of sadness. I'd probably seen the beggar boy for the last time ever. Remembering the old newspaper page that mysteriously appeared from the set of drawers, I pulled out the shoebox from under the bed and look at the headline again.

"BEGGAR BOY KILLED
IN MONTAGUE STREET"

More strongly than before, I felt that the boy that was killed twenty years ago and the boy I had met, and been helped by, were connected. I had to find out more!

Chapter 15

Mum phoned for the doctor in the morning and he arrived just after lunch. After asking me lots of questions, including some about the beggar boy, he brought out a thermometer and checked my temperature. Shining a torch into my eyes he checked for anything wrong. My ears were next to be examined, followed by an examination of my skull and neck.

"Your boy seems fine," he announced to Mum.

Mum asked him, "But what about this boy he claims to have been with?"

"I can't rule out the existence of the boy, and certainly Tommy seems convinced he's been in his company," he said. "But on the other hand, you know what active imaginations young boys have. If you have any more problems don't hesitate to call me again."

The doctor had no sooner left us, when the doorbell rang again. There at the door stood one of the police officers that had nearly knocked me over in the car yesterday. He came inside to talk to Mum and me.

Addressing my Mum he said, "We'd like your boy to come down to the station."

"Is there a problem?" enquired Mum.

"No Madam," said the officer. "We just want to see if there are any grounds for a formal complaint against the boys who chased Tommy on to the road."

"I suppose we'd better go then Tommy," said Mum.

We were escorted into the back of the police car and driven to the station. My curiosity about the death of the boy twenty years ago was playing on my mind.

I asked the policeman, "Do you know anything about the beggar boy who was killed by a car in Montague Street about twenty years ago?"

The policeman shook his head and said, "No that's well before my time. I tell you what though, Sergeant Wilson will probably remember. You can have a word with him."

"Good!" I replied. Maybe I was getting somewhere about finding out the identity of the boy.

Once inside the police station we were led to a small room. After interviewing me for a few minutes, the police seemed satisfied that there was no need to bring a formal complaint against the Dixons. They accepted that it was probably my fault that I ran onto the road, but the Dixons were partly to blame as well.

"The Dixon boys have been warned about their future behaviour and they have promised not to bother you anymore," said the policeman.

Mum nudged me "And I promise not to bother them either," I said.

"Good," said the police officer. "One matter is still puzzling us though."

"What's that?" I said.

"The whereabouts of this beggar boy you spoke of?" said the policeman. "We've had no reports of any beggars in your area for quite some time now."

I gulped and answered, "He said he's leaving – his job is done."

The policeman drew me a strange look and said, "Very well – I suppose that clears up that loose end."

Chapter 15

Mum stood up. "Can we go now?" she asked.

"Yes of course!" said the policeman. "Now stay out of trouble, Tommy."

On our way out of the station I suddenly remembered about Sergeant Wilson. I had to find out if he knew anything about the boy.

I asked at the front desk, "Is there a Sergeant Wilson on duty?"

The policeman smiled and said, "You're looking at him."

"Do you remember about a beggar boy being killed in Montague Street about twenty years ago?" I inquired.

The policeman scratched his head and then said, "As a matter of fact I do. Why do you ask?"

I replied, "I just need to know his name or what he looked like."

"Hold on a minute, I'll go and see if we

have anything on file," said the Sergeant as he went to get the information.

A few minutes later he returned holding a large brown paper envelope.

He explained to me, "We never found out the boy's name. We even had an artist draw his face to try and help our enquiries, but it was no use."

"Can I see the drawing," I asked excitedly.

"Yes it's in here," said the Sergeant as he opened the envelope and placed a sheet of paper in front of me.

A chill ran down my spine as I looked at the drawing. I couldn't believe what I was seeing. It was an exact likeness of the beggar boy who had helped me avenge my humiliations at the hands of my neighbours. The same boy who had saved my life!

I suddenly realised why nobody else had seen the boy apart from me.

The beggar boy must have been a ghost!

We hope you enjoyed this story from the Creepers series. There are six titles for you to collect:

Ghost Writer

The Piano

Beggar Boy

The Scarecrow

Mirror Mirror

The Wishing Well

This series was conceived by Edgar J Hyde and much of the text was provided by his minions under slavish conditions and pain of death! Thankfully none of the minions defied their master and so we can say 'thank you' to them for toughing it out and making this series possible